Temptations of the Flesh Part II It's Personal

Copyright © 2024 by James DeBoris Franklin Sr.

All rights reserved.

Permission to reproduce or transmit in any form or by any means, electronic or mechanical, including photocopying, photographic and recording audio or video, or by any information storage and retrieval system, must be obtained in writing from the author.

Temptations of the Flesh Part II Its Personal is a registered trademark of James DeBoris Franklin Sr.

First printing June 2024

Library of Congress Cataloging-in-Publication Data

DeBoris Franklin Sr, James
temptations of the flesh part II its personal / by james deboris franklin sr.

Paperback ISBN: 9798328868280
Hardcover ISBN: 9798328868396

Printed in the U.S.A.

TEMPTATIONS OF THE FLESH
Part II
"It's Personal"

James DeBoris Franklin Sr.

CONTENTS

INTRODUCTION 1
CHAPTER 1 3
CHAPTER 2 29
CHAPTER 3 49

INTRODUCTION

This story is about life and its consequences. It will show you how experiencing love on a level that is unexplainable to most people can be beautiful as well as tragic. Understand that it's your responsibility to control how you manage the pain and heartache that's been given to you by the person you love the most. The way you react to the questions you seek will cause you to do things that you will regret. God is able ask Him to help you control and clear your thoughts so the decisions you make will bring about a change that will benefit you for life. Love yourself enough to release all things that don't represent loving you. I pray this book helps you see your worth and how important self-love is. Never jeopardize or compromise your love for self to make others feel loved. To God be the glory because without Him none of this would be possible. Enjoy!

Temptations of the Flesh, Part II

"It's Personal"

CHAPTER 1

It's been a year and David's life has become something that he never would have imagined. His life as a single parent with a child that has HIV is overwhelming, but he has no choice but to keep pushing forward. He misses Tina every day but keeps wondering how all of this happened. No one seems to be able to answer any of his questions or concerns. He's determined to find the answer to his question of how their son got HIV when he or Tina were not infected.

Theo is now a year old. David gave his son this name because he was a "divine gift" as that's the meaning of "Theo." David has experienced a level of love he never thought possible. The love for his son is indescribable.

Theo made David grow up faster than he wanted to, but David wouldn't have it any other way. He tried dating but his love and thoughts of Tina hinders him from moving forward with anyone and he's just not ready to introduce Theo to anyone yet, so for now, it's just him and his amazing baby boy...

Damon and Darrius are in a good place or so it seems. Damon is happy with their arrangement, especially now that Billy Ray has ghosted Darrius. Damon never misses a chance to make Darrius feel or look stupid for his interactions with Billy Ray.

James DeBoris Franklin Sr.

The idea of him committing to Darrius is no longer a thought. He has begun to embrace women more than he ever had in the past. He knows that this hurts and bothers Darrius, but he just doesn't care about his feelings.

Damon feels that this is his payback for Darrius' involvement with Billy Ray. He now uses sex as a way of punishing Darrius. He has become very aggressive and rough with him, not giving him an option of how, when, or where it happens. Damon is angry that Darrius chose Billy Ray over him, and his plan is to continue making Darrius pay for the decision he made that caused their relationship to suffer. In Damon's mind, Darrius will spend the rest of his life trying to make up for what happened between him and Billy Ray, but Darrius is on a different level when it comes to Damon. He really doesn't care what Damon is doing because he's waiting for Billy Ray to show up so they can go right back to spending the kind of time he wants. Since Billy Ray has been gone, Darrius has missed him more than he thought he would. He's feeling like there might have been more to them hooking up than he was willing to admit. He starts to wonder if what he is feeling is associated with love or his emotions guiding him to a place that he misses the most when it comes to Billy Ray, his sex. Darrius is reminded of how Billy Ray sexed him every time Damon became aggressive with him. He sees Billy Ray when Damon is doing his so-called

Temptations of The Flesh Part II

"punishment sex," because that's how Billy Ray got his attention.

Damon has no idea that he's really being used, which allows Darrius to continue to feel like Billy Ray is part of his life even though he hasn't heard from him. Between the Damon episodes and struggling with being sick, Darrius is in a good place. Deep down he knows Billy Ray has probably moved on, but all he has are his memories of them and what they had so he will continue to let Damon treat him in that fashion because Damon is playing the game just the way he wants it played. Damon thinks he's in control and that's just the way Darrius wants it.

Mary and Bishop White are just ok: she still has thoughts of leaving him but she's afraid of living life without him. She has given a lot of thought regarding what Billy Ray told her about letting go of the bishop and moving on. Money is not an issue because Billy Ray made sure she'd never have to worry about that. Billy Ray also left her some property that he purchased before he died. He wanted his sister to be happy and to live life without subjecting herself to the bishop's mess.

As for the bishop, he continues to do his thing with members. His church has grown and that means he has more options (members) to pray for. He doesn't seem to care about his wife's feelings or how his congregation views her as their first lady. He has

James DeBoris Franklin Sr.

been doing this for so long that it's just a part of who he is now. Mary, like it or not, will have to deal with it until he decides to stop but that's not going to happen anytime soon.

It was a beautiful, sunny day and Mary was in her feelings as she struggled with knowing why David's son had HIV. She wants to tell him, but she's not sure if she should. She finally decides to go see David to check on him and his son, but while thinking about David and his situation, she also has thoughts about Damon and the what-ifs. Mary knows that her thoughts are not right, but she can't help but wonder what would have happened if she had allowed Damon the opportunity to get close to her. While deep in her thoughts she began to touch herself. She began to fantasize about Damon and what sex would be like with him. This was something that Mary has never entertained before, but she's in a different place right now so she's just going with whatever happens.

The bishop sees Mary and begins to watch her. He automatically assumes that it's him she's thinking of as she pleases herself. If he only knew who has tweaked his wife's mind. The bishop and his strong sex drive replace Mary's hand with his erect penis and started to make love to her, but Mary wasn't making love to her husband she was sexing Damon. She never opened her eyes because she wanted her fantasy to play out the way she had it in her mind. The bishop, knowing how to please his wife was very

Temptations of The Flesh Part II

confident in making her climax and she did, but all the excitement went away when she opened her eyes and saw the bishop looking down at her.

For the first time in her life with the bishop things were off and she felt different. She reflects on the conversation she had with her brother and now she's considering his request to move on without the bishop. Disappointed but satisfied, she proceeded to shower to get dressed for her unexpected visit with David. She reaches out to him and asks if they could meet at the park and talk? David said yes.

Once at the park, it reminded her of the time she met Damon there, so she started to look around hoping to see him. She was startled by David's greeting which was a hug from behind and a kiss on her cheek. He immediately apologized for how he greeted her but explained that it had been a while since he'd seen her and that he was happy she had contacted him. Mary was very emotional.

"What's wrong? Are you ok?" David asked.

"I'm good. I just have a lot going on." Mary replied.

David said, "Do you want to talk about it?"

"No, not now but maybe later."

"Is that why you reached out to me because of what's bothering you?"

"Yes! Kinda."

"Ok, because I have questions that I'd like to have answered but no one seems to be able to help me." David said.

At that moment, Mary became nerves and started to regret trying to check up on him. "What questions David?"

"Questions about Tina and Theo."

"Who is Theo?" Mary asked.

"Oh, I'm sorry that's my son's name."

"Oh! And where is your son?"

"I left him with my mom."

Mary was about to give David the answers to all his questions when David stopped her. He was having a moment. He starts to explain how hard it's been with his son and the circumstances surrounding them. He begins to talk about Tina and how much he misses her while trying to understand what happened. She was supposed to be here with him, they should be raising their son together but it's only him. David said, "I've gotten tested several times to make sure I was ok and every test I've taken has come back negative."

"So, You and Tina didn't have sex once you got back together?" Mary questioned.

"Yes, we had sex, but I promised her I would never put her in that situation again. I should have done

Temptations of The Flesh Part II

what she asked in the beginning, but I didn't and that was the start of our problems. If I had only used the condoms, she might still be here. That was my wake-up call because even though she was pregnant I still used a condom to show her that I had learned my lesson and that I'd never lose her again because of my selfish ways."

David begins to cry, and Mary starts to console him when she noticed Bishop White having a conversation with another woman. They were sitting kind of close to each other but that didn't really bother her. What caught her attention was the kid that was sitting in between them. Normally she would just blow that off, but this was different. She's hoping that it's just a church member but for some reason this hits a little different. Mary asked David if they could continue this conversation later.

"Yes!" David agreed.

Mary approaches the bishop, and he was surprised to see her there.

"Hello love." he says.

"You're not going to introduce me to your member or friend?"

Before he could say anything, she introduces herself.

"My name is Nena and I know all about you First Lady Mary."

"Really! So, you know Bishop White's status, meaning he's married."

"Yes! I know he's married to you and the church but that has nothing to do with me. She said listen I have waited a long time to tell you this. Bishop White and I have been seeing each other for a while now." Nena confessed.

"What's a while?" Mary asked.

"Honestly that's not important but what is important is your husband is the father of my son."

Mary was devastated but her pride wouldn't let her breakdown.

She asked, "Is this true? Is this your child?"

"Yes," the bishop acknowledged

Mary's heart dropped. She couldn't believe that this was happening, but she refused to let this take over her emotions. Mary looked at the bishop and Nena sitting there with their son and walked away. Bishop White tried to stop her, but she kept walking as if he wasn't there. On the outside, she looked strong and unbothered but, on the inside, this had destroyed her.

Bishop turns to Nena full of rage. "Why! Why did you do that? I told you I was going to tell her, but you just had to open your big ass mouth and now you've started something that I may not be able to fix."

Temptations of The Flesh Part II

"Fix? Oh! so you're still trying to keep both of us? You are to blame for all of this. You knew you were married when you approached me. You knew you were married when you laid down with me and you also knew you were married when you were telling me that all you wanted was for me to have your child. That didn't stop you from loving me as if I was your wife. So now she knows the truth about us."

The bishop looked at her in disgust and said, "You're right. This is my fault because I never should have even touched you, but you are just as guilty as I am. You allowed me to be with you knowing that I was married, and it wasn't a problem for you to benefit from all the trips and financial blessing that you were given."

"I was single when I met you and I am still single and yes, I took everything you gave me but let's be honest. I know that I wasn't the only woman you were sleeping with outside of your wife. You created this life for us, so you need to keep doing what you were doing before Mary knew about you and me because I am not going anywhere. Now, go and save your marriage and I will see you later this evening."

Bishop White was angry, but he knew she was speaking the truth. He enjoyed the way his life was, and he didn't want to lose Mary or Nena.

On his way home, he was trying to figure out how to repair his relationship with his wife. He knew it would be difficult, but he also knew that she loved him, so he felt as if he had a chance to get her back. In his heart, he knew Mary was going to leave him.

As he entered the house, he expected Mary to be upset and for their home to be destroyed but Mary was sitting on the couch as if she was waiting for him to come home. He was shocked.

"Have a seat" Mary instructed.

The bishop tried to sit next to her, and she told him to not come near. As he sits down, Mary begins to cry. Once again, the bishop tries to console her, and she tells him not to touch her. Mary begins to explain how disrespectful he has been to her and their marriage and how he has made her look like a fool to the community and their congregation. Mary tells the bishop about the conversation she had with Billy Ray before he died and how Billy Ray wanted her to leave him in fear of what just happened or worse. She went on to tell the bishop that she told her brother that she could not live without him, and that the bishop was all she knew so leaving was not an option; until now.

"I knew marring you would be challenging, and I knew being a man of God would put you in a position where you would have to minister to men as well as women and some of those sessions would be a one on one. But I also thought that you would have been strong enough to handle any temptations of the flesh… along with all situations brought before you, but it's obvious that I was wrong. I loved

Temptations of The Flesh Part II

you enough not to put myself in a position that would degrade you as my husband/the bishop or me as your wife. You've done the most and this really hurt, so from this point on, I will not be sleeping in the same bedroom as you so you can get your things and move them into the guest bedroom. I will continue to support you as the first lady of the church until I decide on what I am going to do. There will be no more love making so do not come near me and I am going to start living my life as I see fit so do not question me as I will not question you. Honestly, we have just become roommates, no more, no less. You have lived the life of a single man all while being married to me so now it's my turn to explore life and all the benefits of it. I hope she was worth all of this because we will never be the same. I could lie and tell you that everything will be ok and to just give me a little time to absorb this but why lie. I am not going to be ok and life as we know it has forever changed and it's all because of you so thank you for opening a door that I would never have opened. I am yours on paper only and that's all I am willing to give you so continue to do your sick and shut in house calls because for the first time in our lives together I do not care where you go or who you are with."

Mary's mindset has shifted, and her passive nature has now become aggressive on all levels. Her thoughts of wanting to see Damon tripled and she wanted the desire she had for him to come true...

James DeBoris Franklin Sr.

Mary calls David to continue their conversation. She asked if she could come over and David replied, "Yes!"

David greets Mary at the door and invites her into his home. She asks if she could meet his son and he told her he wasn't comfortable introducing him to anyone at this time and told her that the only woman he has meet was his mother.

Daivd asked Mary if she was, ok.

Mary responded, "I have seen better days, but this too shall pass."

"Who was that woman with the bishop? And is that his child?"

"I really don't want to talk about that right now. It appears to be complicated, and I am not stable enough to deal with that at this moment." Mary begins to cry.

David put his arms around her and held her, which allowed her to just breathe. He wished he would have had someone to give him this kind of support when he lost Tina, so he was not going to let Mary experience any of those unforgettable and almost unforgiveable feelings.

Mary begins to mumble, "I should have listened to Billy Ray. He told me to leave him alone, but I had to be faithful to my husband and my marriage even though I knew he was not faithful to me."

Temptations of The Flesh Part II

"Wait! You knew the bishop was messing around? You knew he wasn't faithful to you?"

"Of course I knew David, but I was his wife and regardless of what he did, our home and I came first. The bishop has been doing this for a long time and I am sure this is only the beginning of what he has created with the women in this community and his congregation. I loved him. He was my first and I have not experienced anyone but him. I now understand that life will reveal things that you need to see even though you're not ready for the lesson that has been forced on you."

David is speechless.

Mary continues, "I know this is a bit much for you. I really came to talk to you about you and Tina but ended up crying and leaning on your shoulder but thank you for listening and not judging me. You are going to make someone very happy when the time is right."

David replied, "Thank you! Mary, I'm sorry about your situation and I pray things will get better but I'm sure it will. You are an amazing woman and I know you're not looking for mister right, right now but I'm convinced that you will find him."

"Thank you David, but you're right I'm not looking for a mister right. Maybe a mister wrong, but definitely not a mister right."

At that moment, David saw Mary in a different light. He wondered if he approached her what her response would be. He went with is first thought and said, "Mary, I know you're going through something, but I have an attraction for you, and I know I'm young, but I was wondering if we could start a conversation, a relationship that will produce the benefit of getting to know each other a little better. That could possibly lead to something special?"

Mary was blown away; she was not expecting David to come at her like that, but she also was low-key, turned on by his respectful approach. Mary smiled and said, "David I'm tickled that you find me attractive, and I'm also impressed with your word play. We both have a lot going on right now so I'm going to have to decline your offer but just know that you have made me feel so special and wanted. You've given me a feeling that I haven't felt in a long time so thank you. And if I can be honest, you really got my attention with you being the young man that you are, so we'll see what happens."

David walks Mary to her car, he opens her door, gives her a hug, and kisses her forehead as he tells her goodbye. Once again, Mary was caught off guard by David's approach and she thinks to herself *little boy you better be glad you're not older because your ass would in a lot of trouble.* She pulls off with a silly smirk on her face.

Temptations of The Flesh Part II

Meanwhile, Bishop White is trying to save the only relationship he seems to have and that's with Nena. Mary is finished with him. As he arrives back at the park, he notices Nena walking with a man that he had never seen before. He stopped her and asked if everything was ok.

"Yes! Why wouldn't it be?" Nena asked.

Bishop White said, "I saw you talking to this person that I have never seen before so I was just making sure you were good. You're not going to introduce me to your friend?"

Nena started to respond and the man she was with cut her off and said, "My name is Damon! What's up Bishop White?"

Bishop White said, "Ok it's obvious you know who I am. Now help me understand who you are and how I might know you?"

"Truth be told you don't know me and the only reason I know who you are is because…"

Nena starts to yell at Damon telling him to shut up, but Damon wasn't hearing that, so he continues to tell the bishop how he knows him.

Damon tells Bishop White, "The reason why I know who you are is because we have been sleeping with the same woman, Nena for years." Bishop White looked at Nena as if he wanted to hurt her. He couldn't believe what he was hearing.

James DeBoris Franklin Sr.

Bishop White said, "Is this true Nena? Have you been sleeping with the both of us? I can't believe you have had my son around this man."

"Hold up! Your son? She told me he was my son. Nena! Am I this child's father? Do you even know who the father is?" Damon questioned.

Bishop White starts to explode with anger. "You allowed me to think that I was the only man you were seeing, and I ruined my marriage thinking you had given me a son, my first and only child, to find out that you lied to me?"

Damon responds, "No! She lied to us. I have been taking care of this little guy ever since he's been in this world. I went to her doctor's visits. I was at the gender reveal party. I was at the hospital when he was born and now, I understand why you wouldn't let me sign the birth certificate. you didn't know who the father was."

Bishop White added, "I did all of that too so you had two different events so we both could be a part of them? Wow! I can't believe you played me, and you were so quick to tell Mary who you were and that this was my son when you been kicking it with this guy for as long as we've been seeing each other."

"Look bishop," Damon started, "when you would come over for your daily visits, after you left, she would call me to come over and finish what you started. She told me that she was going to get

Temptations of The Flesh Part II

everything you had to give her because she knew it was only temporary because you were married. She said she was going to make you think he was your child so you would continue to put money in her hands for your son. All the while, reassuring me that he was my biological son. Well now I want a paternity test. I need to know if I am his father."

Bishop White requested one as well.

"Nena! I hope you and Damon can find happiness together because I am done."

"Bishop! get out of your feelings. You know we are not done, and I will be waiting on you tomorrow for our weekly visit and do not be late." Nena exclaimed.

Bishop White responded, "Damon do you hear her? Are you good with what she is saying?"

"Hey man I really don't care because she was just a Kool pop to me."

"A Kool pop? What is a Kool pop!" Bishop White replied.

"Yes! A Kool pop! A Kool pop is a woman who you enjoy going on dates and having drinks with, someone who you like hanging out with but also know that she'll never be the one you'll commit to. She'll always be the girl you can kick it with but never nothing serious so that makes her a Kool piece of pussy, a Kool pop!"

James DeBoris Franklin Sr.

"Well damn! I have lost everything over a damn Kool pop!" Bishop White walks away disappointed and frustrated. He never thought things would turn out like this.

Damon, Nena, and the child leave together.

Damon didn't care about none of that. He was on a mission, and he wasn't going to let these series of events stop him from getting what he wanted; to lay Nena down and make her body tremble with pleasure. Damon got what he wanted. It was mission accomplished now it's on to the next.

As Damon was leaving Nena's house, he knew he had to go home and deal with Darrius. It was very likely that Darrius was going to want some, but he was tired from having sex with Nena. So, he had to kill some time so he would be ready to handle Darrius when he got home.

Damon goes to a local restaurant and sits at the bar before ordering his drink. He sees Mary sitting at the end of the bar. He was so excited to see her that he moved to be closer to her.

"Hello! Do you remember me?" Darius says.

As Mary turned to see who he was, she couldn't believe it was him. "Yes! I remember you, Damon."

Damon was surprised that she remembered him. "Okay, I have been looking for you for a long time

Temptations of The Flesh Part II

and I clearly remember the day we met but I never got your name so if I may ask, what's your name?"

"My name is Mary."

"I can now put a name to that beautiful face. It's nice to meet you Mary."

"It's nice to see you again Damon. You know, I have a confession."

"And what is your confession?"

"I have been looking for you also. I have been going to the park hoping to find you there so we could continue our conversation and maybe take you up on your offer for dinner."

Damon smiles. "I would love to take you to dinner and continue our conversation."

Damon has forgotten about Darrius and going home to please him. He's so turned on by Mary and her desire to spend time with him that at this point, nothing matters. The thought of him spending time with Billy Ray's wife and the possibility of having sex with her is all he needs to start the revenge process of Billy Ray.

Mary steps out of her comfort zone and tells Damon, "I might want a little more than dinner from you."

Damon couldn't believe what he was hearing, and he really didn't know how to take this because he's usually the aggressive one but going with the flow he asked, "And what might that be Mary?"

"If you have to ask then we might need to cancel the whole date."

"I never want to assume what someone is saying so for me it's better to just ask so we both will have a better understanding of what's going to happen or what that person wants to happen. That way, there won't be any disappointments but after your response I totally understand, and I am looking forward to spending quality as well as pleasurable time with you Mary."

Mary was just as excited as Damon because she is finally going to get the chance to experience him in the flesh and not her thoughts. However, Damon is on another level. He is excited because of the payback to Billy Ray. Mary has no idea she's just another Kool pop for Damon because he has no desire to be with her other than to expose her husband (Billy Ray) for sleeping with his partner, but only after he sleeps with her.

Damon asks Mary for her phone number so they can keep in touch with each other, and Mary gives it to him. Neither wanted to leave so they stayed and continued to have drinks and enjoy each other's company. Just as they started to get comfortable, Darrius walks in. Damon sees him first and tells Mary that he had to leave but will call her to set up a day and time for their date. Mary was shocked at

Temptations of The Flesh Part II

how quickly Damon left but understood that things happen. She finished her drink and thought to herself *today was difficult, but it turned out to be eventful. I am looking forward to seeing, feeling, kissing, and maybe even sucking what Damon has to offer. It's now playtime for the first lady.*

Mary reaches her car and notices that she has several missed calls. She starts to smile because this has never happened to her before. They were from David, Damon, and an uncountable amount from the bishop.

She calls Damon and says, "What's up! I thought you were done for the night."

"Done! Honey, I'm just getting started. Listen, I really want to spend some quality time with you, and I really don't think that we should allow more time to come between us. So, I was wondering how would you feel about spending the night with me? I know that this is kind of sudden, but we've been vibing all night and I was hoping that we could close out the night with you looking up at me while I'm deep inside of you. Or you on top of me riding me cowgirl style while I'm slapping that ass" Damon offered.

Mary responded, "Wow! That's interesting and inviting but what about me looking down at you while you are looking up at me with your mouth and tongue stimulating my clit?"

"Absolutely!"

Mary laughed and said, "I think I'm going to wait and allow things to calm down a little bit because I don't want to be just another woman you lay with for sex and sex only. I'm not saying that we won't ever get there but I can tell you we won't explore those positions tonight so enjoy yourself and whoever you're going to get with tonight. I don't know much about you, but I am sure that the energy you have built up for me will be released in someone else tonight. Good night Damon!"

Mary couldn't see giving herself to Damon even though she knew she only wanted sex to satisfy her need to get back at the bishop. She wanted to control the process of giving her goods to someone and Damon was mad aggressive so she knew he would possibly be a problem. He was one of three options for her: the other was the bishop and that was not going to happened, so she was left with David. She knew he was young and kind of vulnerable so controlling him wouldn't be hard to do. She felt that he would enjoy and appreciate the act of visiting her private and secluded island that only one person ever inhabited. Mary, being horny, calls David.

"Hello! Mary are you ok?" David asked.

"Yes, I'm good, I know it's late, but can I come see you? I need your help with a little problem I'm having."

Temptations of The Flesh Part II

"Yes! I'll be here waiting for you." David responded.

Damon wasn't upset with Mary's decision because he knew his time with her was coming. Mary was just another option added to his list for his satisfaction when he needed it. More importantly, he knew he had his in-house ass at home, and it was all his all the time. He thought *Mary was right. I'm about to fulfill this need for aggression, frustration, and anger with a bit of revenge for Billy Ray. Darrius will reap the benefit of what Mary was supposed to get tonight. And since it's him, I must punish him for what he did to me with Billy Ray. He will experience a lot of pain with little pleasure, and I hope he understands that he brought this on himself. I'm sure it really won't matter to him. I believe he likes it when I call myself punishing him because he seems to be at peace each time we finish.*

Darrius walked in the house and Damon was waiting for him.

"Where have you been? I've been waiting on you." Damon questioned.

"Stop it! I saw you at the bar talking to some lady but it's cool. I'm not going to reveal who you are to anyone. I just needed to get out of the house for a minute, so I decided to go have a drink and socialize a little bit and guess who I saw at the bar doing what he does best? You! Damon, why did you leave? You left her sitting there looking crazy because of how you chose to leave. You act like you were in a

James DeBoris Franklin Sr.

relationship and you were about to get caught but let me remind you that we are roommates who have meaningless sex from time to time and that's the good and bad of our bond so enjoy being yourself because I have accepted who and what you are" Darrius said.

Damon heard Darrius but having sex and releasing all his built-up pressure on him is the only thing that's on his mind. Damon tells Darrius, "Thank you for accepting me for who and what I am. Having said that, understand I'm in need of you pleasing me so go to my room. As you walk over there get undressed. And once you're in my room, turn on some music, pick whatever song you feel is appropriate for this moment. Once you've done that get comfortable and think of the position you enjoy the most and then relax and clear your mind. Allow your thoughts to fit the experience we are about to share."

Darrius did everything Damon asked. He had set his mind and the mood for him and Billy Ray to have an amazing night. Damon is so caught up with himself that he really believes Darrius loves him when honestly, Darrius is using him to get what he can't have from Billy Ray. Damon is Billy Ray every time they have sex and Darrius is completely satisfied because he's sexing and loving Billy Ray not Damon. But tonight, Darrius has a surprise for Damon: this will be a night that he will never forget.

Temptations of The Flesh Part II

As Damon walks into the room, Darrius sees that he has an erection that seems to be a little different, a little bigger and a little harder. He was a little worried that Damon was going to be a little extra in trying to get his point across about Billy Ray, but as Darrius began to think about Billy Ray and the way he use to sex him, it really didn't matter what Damon did because to Darrius, Billy Ray had come back to him.

Darrius started doing things that Damon had never seen him do. Darrius was making sounds and pleasing him in ways he had never done before. Damon was about to reach his peak and started saying Darrius's name and, in the moment, Darrius says, "Cum for me! I've missed you so much!"

That made Damon feel as if they were back to how it was in the beginning and Damon wanted to show Darrius that he missed him too.

Damon was in a place he hadn't been with Darrius in a long time, and it felt good to be close and connected with him again. He was so pleased and overcome with what was happening that he no longer had thoughts of revenge for Billy Ray. He gave in to Darrius like never before and just as Damon was releasing his uncontrollable rush on Darrius, he began to scream out Darrius's name. Darrius's, without any regards or regrets for Damon's feelings says, "No one put that loving on me like you do Billy Ray! I love you! you and only you!"

Darrius looked at Damon as Damon's eyes began to fill with tears.

Darrius said, "Why are you crying? I gave you what you wanted. You wanted to punish me every time we had sex but what you fail to realize is that Billy Ray and I were always on that level. So, I used you to get what I needed just as you were using me to get your so-called revenge. I gave it to you differently this time so you will have an insight into what I did with Billy Ray. Now you can continue to give yourself to these women who will never make you call their names like I've made you scream mine tonight."

Damon was blown away. His pride was shattered because he got played by Darrius and never saw it coming. This angered Damon to the degree that he wanted to destroy and humiliate Darrius on all levels, but he couldn't do it without exposing himself. So, he decided to do it by bring all his female friends and dates to the apartment. He's going to make Darrius listen to him having sex and entertain other women as often as he wants and the first and only person, he's thinking of is Mary. Yes! Mary will be the one to make Darrius hate what he did to him or so he thinks. But if I was Damon, I wouldn't count on it.

CHAPTER 2

Mary arrives at Daivd's house and David asks, "Are you ok? What's going on? The bishop didn't hit you, did he?"

"No! My problem is kind of personal and I'm a little uncertain about it, but at this moment I can't lie, I need it. So, what I want and/or need from you is some no strings attached sex."

David instantly got hard. Mary sees how excited he was through his shorts.

"Damn! I'm sorry for cussing but I didn't think you was working with that."

David began to pull down his shorts and Mary couldn't believe how large he was. She quickly asked, "Where is your mom?"

"She's at her man's place" David replied.

David took Mary's hands and placed them on his penis. Mary was impressed with the size of it and began to slowly stroke it. She begins to reflect on her declining David's suggestion of having a conversation relationship because now she wanted to have a conversation with his penis, but she began to think about Tina and what happened to her and her having HIV.

She stops and asks David again, "Are you sure you are not infected?"

David shows her his results from all the tests he has taken. "I am not going to enter you unprotected. I will put on a condom before anything like that happens."

Mary was still a little uncomfortable, but she wanted to see what it was like to be with someone other than the bishop. David led Mary into his bedroom, and it was dead silent.

"Aren't you going to turn some music?" Mary asked.

As David was closing the door he replied, "Normally I would but the only sounds I want to hear are the sounds of you being pleased. Your moans and you softly saying my name."

"So, you think I'm going to call your name?" Mary questioned.

"No! I know you're going to because I'm a pleaser and I get excited and turned on by making you do and say things that you never thought you would. That's where me being young will be an advantage for me and you."

"Really? Explain."

"You are going to get a different kind of pleasure tonight." David removes his shorts and starts to undress Mary.

Temptations of The Flesh Part II

Mary grabs his extremely hard penis and begins to squeeze and pull on it at the same time. David kisses Mary on her neck and slowly moves to her breast and sucks on her nipples. With every kiss her nipples got harder. While kissing and caressing Mary's body David could see that she was enjoying it.

David tells Mary to open her legs. His touch was gentle, and that helped Mary become more comfortable. As he continued to touch her, he felt her body relax. The spot on her body that he was caressing with his hands he now replaced with his mouth.

David started giving Mary oral sex and because he was a pleaser, he paid attention to the way Mary's body accepted what he was doing to her. He started to hear her moan and that turned him on even more. While he was tasting her, he put on a condom. David wanted to see Mary's expression when he first penetrated her but before he could enter her, Mary softly says, "I'm Cumming! Please don't stop!"

David continued to give her what she asked for but then he decided to penetrate her. Her body started to shake and David slowly pushed as much as Mary could take inside of her. Daivd asked Mary if she was ok, and Mary never said a word but started to throw it back at David. She started moving her hips and body in a manner that surprised her, but she couldn't stop. She told David not to hold back, she wanted all of it. David pushed everything he had inside of her. Mary was experiencing something totally different, but she loved it. Mary started to talk to David.

"You said I was going to call your name but I'm going to make you scream mine as you're cumming. I must admit, you got some damn good loving to be so young, but I just need to show you that you can't handle this grown woman's playground."

"You talk too much and now I'm going to make you say my name!" David takes Mary's legs and starts to put them on his shoulders but he thought about all the shit she had just said. So instead, he placed them behind her head so that she would feel every inch of him. He let one of her legs go and it landed on his shoulder. He put his hand around her throat, he gave it a soft squeeze. Her eyes started to roll so David's stroke became more aggressive.

David pulled her to the edge of the bed and told her to put her arms around his neck. He stood up with her and watched her as she bounced on him. He noticed she started to shake again so he placed her back on the bed and while she was experiencing what seem to be an orgasm, he continued to please her until he heard her say, "David I can't take anymore." That made David want to release with Mary. That's when David gave Mary a different kind of stroke, a stroke that was much faster, harder, and more aggressive. It appeared to be uncontrollable,

Temptations of The Flesh Part II

but David was about to explode. He wanted Mary to remember this night so with his last thrust he strongly says her name, "Mary! I'm cumming!"

Mary heard him and began to move her body in a way that would help him have an awesome feeling of relief. Mary thought she didn't have any more to give but wanted to make David scream her name. She became so heated that he gave her another orgasm and when Daivd called her name, she screamed his. The climax between the two of them was amazing.

Afterwards, Mary and David lay stretched out on his bed in disbelief of what had just happened. Mary said, "This is something that was not supposed to happen, but I have no regrets David and I can promise you this will not be the last time we get together. This is the start of our conversation relationship we just reap the benefits first."

David laughed and said, "Mary! You were amazing and yes this will not be our last time. I know we must keep it on the low and I'm good with that. I really enjoyed you and I'm glad you chose me."

As Mary was leaving, David noticed something different about her. It was her walk. David said, "What's up with your walk? You seem to be walking funny are you alright?"

"You're tripping and yes, I'm good. There is nothing wrong with the way I walk."

James DeBoris Franklin Sr.

David smiled and said, "Yeah ok but your walk is different now from when you first got here."

"You're feeling yourself, aren't you? It was good but stop thinking you seeing something that you're not. My walk is the same."

Mary kisses David. As she gets in her car, she tells him that she will call him later in the day. As she drove off, she began to laugh. She was so embarrassed. David was right, her legs were weak from their unforgettable love session. She tried hard to hide it but couldn't. Her legs were still trembling, and she was still leaking from what David had caused her to release. She felt like she was still having a mini orgasm. No words could explain what had just happened and she knew she would be going back for more. *If this was what the bishop was getting on the side, I can kind of understand why he keep going back. We have never had anything close to what David put on me tonight. Our love making was good, but it does not compare to what I got tonight. Love wasn't invited to my encounter tonight which is ok. I didn't need love, I needed to be fucked. I know I shouldn't be thinking like this, but I've been a good girl all my life which made me a good wife. I have never done anything remotely close to this because I was taught that a good woman represents her family by how she presents herself to others and I respected my family, church, and husband very well despite his actions. My experiences in life are limited. I'm not trying to*

Temptations of The Flesh Part II

make up for lost time, but I am going to enjoy every bit of what I've started. I deserve to be happy and that is my motivation. If happiness looks and feels anything like tonight every time you see me, I'll be smiling.

Mary's phone keeps lighting up and she just knew it was the bishop calling because it was so late, but it wasn't, it was Damon. He had called several times and had left plenty of voice mails, but Mary was tired and didn't feel like dealing with him. So, she ignored his attempts to contact her.

Mary knew she had to deal with the bishop when she got home and it was going to take everything in her to handle him and his questions. When Mary walked into the house, she was taken by surprise with the bishop and what he had tried to put together for her. He had lights and candles that had melted and dinner that had gotten cold. He had fallen asleep on the couch waiting for Mary to come home. She covered him up with a blanket and went into her room to get ready for bed.

Mary couldn't help but think about David and the way he made her lose her composure. He gave her a level of sex that she really enjoyed. She couldn't stop thinking about how wonderful it felt to experience someone who made her feel whole, wanted, and sexy. David had taken her to a place she never thought existed and she didn't want anything or anybody to come between them because she was caught up in her feelings for David. Mary wanted David all to herself, but she didn't want him to feel crowded, so she figured she'd played it cool until she was ready to tell him how she truly felt.

A new day dawned, and Mary woke up with so much joy. The bishop woke up to hearing her singing and he thought that she was in a better place so now might be the best time to try and get her back. He turned the doorknob to the bedroom, and it was locked. He knocked on the door and Mary didn't answer. He could hear her moving around so he asked if he could come in so they could talk.

"We have nothing to talk about bishop." Mary's phone began to ring.

The bishop asked, "Who's calling you?"

Mary responded, "I owe you no answer to any questions you might have, as of yesterday. You showed me what I was worth to you and as hard as it was for me to believe what was happening the truth was exposed and I had no choice but to take that punch to the face and keep moving. I was hurt and embarrassed by the man I gave my all to. You were supposed to protect me from all harm, but you were the one who initiated it and now you want me to get over it so we can move on. Know that we will never be the same and I'm going to do what I want from this point on. I would advise you to be careful about the questions you ask because you might not be ready to hear my answer. Little sweet Mary is

Temptations of The Flesh Part II

gone, and will I never be that woman again. You destroyed her with your inappropriate acts as The Bishop and your weekly sick and shut in visits."

Mary opens the door, and the bishop was blown away with how beautiful she looked.

"Where are you going" asked the bishop.

"Are you sure you want to know bishop? I will tell you this it's not to visit the sick and shut in." Mary noticed the time and said, "You usually would've been gone on your visits by now. Everything is understood, and you should feel good because you are now free to continue with your healing and blessing sessions. Please don't let me be the reason you stop blessing this community with your weekly visits."

The bishop knows she's being sarcastic, but he can't blame her for it. He knows he really messed up and now realizes that getting her back is going to be more difficult than he thought. He watched his wife leave the house looking and smelling good with no idea of where she was going. This hit him hard because for the first time, he could see how Mary felt when he left to do his weekly visits. He tries to call her and apologizes for everything, but she wouldn't answer. Mary was not about to allow him to ruin her mood, so she ignored his calls.

Mary calls Damon back and invites him to brunch. He accepts with excitement.

Damon starts to realize that this was his chance to get back at Darrius, so he asked Mary if she would be open to having brunch at his place. She agreed. He sent her his address and began to prepare their meal. Darrius smells something cooking and asks Damon what was he doing?

"I'm having company so I'm making us something to eat" Damon replied.

"Company! You're bringing your date here?" Darrius questioned.

"Yes, I am, and she will be the first of many."

"So, she knows you go both ways?" Darrius asked.

"What's up with all these questions? All you need to know is that I'm having a female visitor, and this is going to be a regular thing from this point on" Damon stated.

"Ok! And judging by the way you responded, I'm willing to bet she doesn't know but she will I can promise you that."

As Damon began to walk towards Darrius the doorbell rang. "You better keep your mouth shut!" Damon demanded.

Darrius goes into his room and Damon opens the door. He couldn't believe how beautiful Mary looked. He was stunned.

"Are you going to invite me in" Mary asked.

Temptations of The Flesh Part II

Damon replied, "Yes! I'm sorry come in please."

Mary complimented his home and asked what was for brunch. Damon said, "I'm cooking bacon, eggs, pancakes, and a little fruit to make this meal as beautiful as you are. A glass of mimosa will compliment it."

Mary replied, "That sounds good. I haven't had anyone to cook for me outside of my husband."

"Really! Well, I hope you like it and if you do, maybe we can make this a regular thing" Damon offered.

"Maybe, but if you can't cook, you get no dessert."

Damon thought to himself. *I'm getting that dessert and then some.*

"Ok! I can live with that" he said aloud.

As they began to eat, Darrius came out of his room and said, "Damon what are you cooking? It smells so good. Oh! I didn't know you had company, please introduce me to your friend.

Damon gave Darrius the most hated look and said, "Mary this is Darrius and Darrius this is Mary."

Darrius greeted Mary and returned to his room. Mary asked Damon why he didn't tell her he had a roommate. Damon replied, "We share this apartment and we've been friends for a long time. To be honest it's cheaper living like this. I apologize for not telling you."

James DeBoris Franklin Sr.

"I understand because my husband and I have become roommates so yes, I get it."

"So how was your meal?" Damon asked.

"It was good."

"Dessert good?"

"Yes, dessert good" Mary confirmed.

Damon asked Mary if they could go to his room. She said yes but Damon wasn't ready for what was about to happen. All Mary wanted was some head, a little bit of that oral sex and nothing else. But Damon was going for it all. This was his night, and it was going to be epic. It was his chance to get back at Billy Ray by fucking his wife and letting Darrius hear it. He couldn't have asked for a better set up.

Damon begins to touch and caress Mary. He unbuttons her pants and tries to kiss her, but Mary wouldn't let him, so he starts kissing her neck. He began to pull her pants down and Mary notices his penis had gotten hard. He started taking off his clothes and she thought to herself, *you are much smaller than David*, but she allowed him to continue. He pulled her pants off and slowly removed her panties. He kissed her body as he stroked his penis. He began to kiss her private place. He noticed that her clit had gotten hard and that turned him on even more. He started licking, kissing, and sucking on her clit trying to make her have an orgasm. Mary didn't seem to be close to

Temptations of The Flesh Part II

having an orgasm, so his thought was, *I'm not getting any pleasure doing what I'm doing so I'm going to try and penetrate her.* Mary wasn't having it she stopped him, and he got fighting mad.

"What's wrong with you? Why are you acting like this? Why are you mad because I won't let you penetrate me? I don't know you like that and you don't even have enough respect for me to use a condom. What's up with that?" Mary asked.

"A condom! I put my mouth on you and you talking about a condom? I'm clean and disease free but you're worried about me using a condom. You need to be worried about your husband and his no condom wearing ass." Damon snapped.

"What are you talking about? How do you know my husband?" Mary asked.

Damon said, "I know your husband probably better than you do."

Mary was starting to get upset so she asked, "What do you know about my husband?"

"I know Billy Ray with his sorry ass" Damon answered.

"Billy Ray!" Mary exclaimed.

"Yes Billy Ray!" Damon confirmed.

"Billy Ray is not my husband he's, my brother." Mary begins to put her clothes back on and starts to

James DeBoris Franklin Sr.

think about the lifestyle Billy Ray lived before he died, and she asked, "How do you know my brother."

Before Damon could answer, Darrius was knocking on his door. He said, "I couldn't help but overhear you say that you're Billy Ray's sister?"

Damon goes off, "Why in the hell are you listening to my conversation with my company. You need to find you something to do and stay out of my business."

"Damn you, Damon! I want to know why Billy Ray hasn't reached out to me. I've been waiting for him to come back to me and I haven't heard anything from him. Is he ok?" Darrius asked.

Mary put two and two together and realized that Darrius was someone Billy Ray had been with to spread his rage throughout the LGBTQ community. Damon was on the downlow. Mary was disgusted with Damon and how he tried to play her. She thought, *what if I had allowed him to sex me the way he wanted to?* She could have possibly been exposed to the very disease that killed her brother.

Mary told Darrius that Billy Ray was good, and that he had relocated but she would tell Billy Ray he asked about him. This made Darrius happy. It gave him hope that he and Billy Ray could possibly have a future together. Mary knew that Billy Ray was never coming back and Darrius as well as Damon

Temptations of The Flesh Part II

could have some health issues in the future. Mary gathers up her things and begins to walk out. Damon hasn't caught on that Mary knows about him and his identity, so he continues to ask her for sex.

"I am good," Mary says, "and this will never happen again. You should be ashamed of yourself. You swing both ways and you're ok putting others in harm's way for your own personal pleasure. You are playing with people's lives, and it's clear that you don't care but your day is coming. I just ask when it hits you, please remember this day. The day you could have scared me for life knowing who and what you are. I pray no one has fallen for your mess. Lose my number, because this is finished."

Damon tries to explain to her, but Mary is done with this encounter. This has opened her eyes to how easily your life can change overnight. She's now thinking about the bishop, everything he has done, and the things he might still be doing. She decides that it's time to get checked out before she allows anyone to touch her again. Mary knows the bishop has a child and she's not the mother, so anything is possible.

While on her way home, the bishop calls and starts to apologize to her. Mary stops him and says, "I'm on my way home and we need to talk. I need you to be honest with me so find it in your heart to tell me the truth regardless of how it might affect me."

James DeBoris Franklin Sr.

"I will tell you the truth about anything you ask."

"Okay! I'll see you shortly."

As she drives home, Mary begans to think about David and what she could have possibly given him but that would be a conversation they would have after her talk with the bishop and the results of her test. Her thoughts of Billy Ray and the conversation they had before he died has become a real-life situation. She realizes that what she's doing to try and get back at the bishop isn't her. She understands how close she came to experiencing something that she never gave thought to until Billy Ray died. She now knows a decision must be made for her protection as well as her peace. Unfortunately, the chances of the bishop getting his wife back has ultimately been depleted.

As Mary arrives home, the bishop was standing on the porch waiting for her. He tried to greet her with a kiss, but Mary pushed him away. Mary proceeds to the living room where she takes a seat on the sofa. She asked the bishop to have a seat in the chair that was across from her.

"Talk!" Mary says.

The bishop wasn't comfortable with Mary's tone and her body language, so he suggested that they go to the park and have an adult conversation about everything. He was hoping that the park had people

Temptations of The Flesh Part II

in it just in case Mary started acting crazy. Mary knew he was stalling but she agreed to go.

Once at the park, they began to talk but in the midst of their conversation, Mary noticed Nena talking to Damon. Nena had also noticed the bishop and Mary and starts to walk towards them. Damon tries to stop her, but she wasn't having it. Nena pulls away from Damon and steps to the bishop and says, "Where have you been and what happened to you last night? You know we were supposed to hook up because we are no longer a secret. Your wife knows about you and me so what's up with you not showing up?"

Before the bishop could answer Mary laughed and said, "Girl you better be careful with that one."

Nena says, "Careful! Girl, I have been messing with Damon for just as long as I have been messing with your husband."

Mary said, "Oh my God! Damon, does she know?"

Nena and the bishop respond, "Know what?"

The bishop asked, "Wait a minute how do you know this man, Mary?"

"I know her brother Billy Ray." Damon answered.

"Billy Ray? And how do you know Billy Ray?" The bishop asks.

James DeBoris Franklin Sr.

"Let's just stop!" Mary insists. "I know Damon because I was going to use him to get back at you for what you did with Nena so earlier today, I allowed him to give me some head."

"What the fuck you say? You let him eat your pussy?" The bishop yelled.

"Calm your ass down or have you forgotten you have a son with this woman. At least I didn't let him penetrate me. And let me get this straight: Nena is sleeping with the both of you and Damon has been with her the same length of time that you have. So, whose baby, is it? Does she even know? Wow! This is crazy I can't believe this is happening but ok. Bishop you and I really need to talk, and I would advise you Nena to get tested as soon as possible. Let's go bishop."

As Mary and the bishop walk off, she told him that he has put them in an unhealthy situation because Damon has a roommate whose name is Darrius. "Darrius is someone that Billy Ray slept with while experiencing his rage of resentment and I found out today that Damon and Darrius are on the downlow. You have been sleeping with this woman for years and so has Damon. He might be infected because of the relationship he has with Darrius, so if he's infected there's a chance that we are as well because of your infidelity. We need to get tested, and I pray it comes back negative."

Temptations of The Flesh Part II

Nena heard what Mary said but she figured Mary was being messy. Nena and Damon went back to her place to give him what Mary couldn't - an orgasm.

CHAPTER 3

David was blowing up Mary's phone but she wasn't answering. He began to worry about her because it's been weeks since he heard from her. Mary didn't want to talk to or see David until her results came back.

Bishop White hasn't preached a sermon since Mary found out about his affair with Nena. Mary has also stopped attending church because of her action with David. She feels guilty about allowing her flesh to be tempted but she really enjoyed David and she just can't stop thinking about him.

Her phone rings and it's the doctor's office informing her that her results are in, and she can come pick them up. Mary is excited and nervous, but she is about to get the answer she's been waiting for. She tells the bishop their results are in, and they need to go pick them up.

Once they arrived at the doctor's office, Mary asked if she could talk to the doctor alone. This made the bishop feel some type of way, but he didn't make a scene. Mary came out full of joy because her results were negative and so were the bishop's. They both were very happy, and the bishop wanted to celebrate the good news by taking his wife to dinner, but Mary wasn't feeling that. The bishop wasn't ready for what was about to happen.

"I have never experienced anything like this in my life and I never thought you would have mistreated me the way you have. I forgive you for it all, but I no longer want to be your wife. I have dealt with hurt and pain from the man I love, and I refuse to continue to live like this, so I want a divorce" Mary said.

Bishop White is stunned. He can't believe that she has just asked him for a divorce. The bishop replied, "Mary please can we just try and talk about this. I do not want to lose you. Look, I know I have made a lot of mistakes, but I love you. I can't and don't want to live without you so can we please try to fix this?"

"A mistake is something that happens once. After that it's a choice. And you made a lot of choices that affected me and our marriage. You have been having sex with at least one woman for years and the two of you have created a child. Unbeknownst to you, she was sleeping with a man who enjoys the company of men and women. You fed me untruths when you came home and gave me what you had already given someone else earlier that day. I must admit though I saw it, but I played dumb and looked over it. The smell of her perfume. The lipstick stain on your shirt collar and the cum spots I saw on your underwear when I washed your clothes. Yes, I knew it, but I didn't want to believe it. Trust and believe God will show you what you need to see. You just got to be willing to accept it when HE shows it to you. I wasn't, but I am now. I don't want anything

Temptations of The Flesh Part II

from you. Billy Ray left me well off so I'm leaving you with everything. You introduced me to a life that I want nothing to do with. Billy Ray died from AIDS, and he warned me about you, but I wouldn't listen. My love for you could have given me the same outcome as my brother and that's death. So, for the first time in my life I'm choosing me over you."

Mary pulls in the driveway of their home and tells the bishop she'll be back to get her things. "I love you bishop, but I love me more."

The bishop gets out of the car feeling hurt and disgusted with himself, but he couldn't argue with anything Mary said and as much as he didn't want to let her go, he knew it was the right thing to do.

"I love you too and I understand" the bishop said.

Mary now feels like a new woman. The weight of everything that has happened has been lifted. She called David and asked if they could talk. He quickly agreed.

Mary is a little disturbed about the conversation that she and David need to have. She's not sure how he's going to receive it, but she knows she must be honest with him and what she knows about Billy Ray and Tina.

Mary is excited to see David. She missed him so much, but she was trying to be cool about it. David grabs Mary and starts to kiss her and she kisses him back. She almost lost sight of what she needed to talk to him about. Mary asked him to stop because she needed to talk to him, and it was important.

David stopped and asked, "What's going on Mary? I haven't heard from you in weeks and now we need to talk. I've missed you so much. Just tell me if you're trying to end us."

"No! I want you. I do not want to lose you, but I need to tell you about something that has happened" Mary says.

"Ok! What is it? What happened?"

"I have asked the bishop for a divorce, and I let Damon give me head."

"What!"

"I know you're mad but please don't be. I was trying to get back at the bishop and I know it was wrong, but I didn't care I just wanted him to hurt like I was, but it didn't work and I'm the one who's looking like a fool. I'm asking you to forgive me, David. I didn't realize how much I cared for you until all of this happened but now, I have no doubts about being with you and only you. Can you find it in your heart to forgive me?"

David looked at her with tears rolling down his face and said, "I've been through so much at this young age: losing Tina and my son being sick; not being able to go to college, so yeah, my life has been hard, but it was all before you. You have given me the type

Temptations of The Flesh Part II

of hope and understanding that me and my son can have love and happiness in our lives, so yes, I can forgive you because I want to be with you too."

Mary tells him that he has made her happy and she has a surprise for him.

"What is it."

"I want you and Theo to move in with me because I want you and I to be a couple" Mary says. "We will have to keep it on the low until my divorce is finalized but I can promise you it will be worth it. So, are you ok with that?"

David was blown away, because all he's ever heard was do not move into a woman's house because that gives her power over you, and she can control how long you can stay and when she wants you to leave because it's her house not yours. But David didn't see that in Mary. He saw her hurt and pain that was brought on by her husband's infidelities. She just needed someone who could show her genuine love, respect, and honesty to help her get through this.

"Yes absolutely! Thank you for accepting and loving me and my child enough to even offer this to us" David said.

"I do accept everything that comes with the both of you and I am more than willing to assist you in raising your son."

James DeBoris Franklin Sr.

Even though Mary had strong feelings for David, she knew at some point things would become challenging. Mary also felt a little guilty because she knows why his son has AIDS and she feels obligated in a way because it was her brother who caused all of this. Her feelings for David are real, and she knows they will continue to grow for him.

Mary's life is and will be very different now. No more first lady of the church. No more living the life of a preacher's wife. Divorced! And now, the owner of her own home and the freedom to be and love whomever she chooses.

Meanwhile, the bishop has come to realize that he has destroyed his marriage with his sinful ways. He reflects back to when Mary, almost caught him and Tina in one of his counseling sessions and how close he was to having sex with her. The outcome of that would have been horrible and now Mary knows he has a child with another woman. He also realizes how lucky he has been not to have contracted any disease which he could have transferred to his wife who did not deserve any of this. He understands he must take accountability for his actions, because he does not like the man that he's become. His reality is that he has caused his soon-to-be-divorced wife, the church, and his community a lot of humiliation and embarrassment. He knows he must come clean with everything and that's what he's preparing to do. He has planned for Sunday's service to be about being open and honest, about the pain and hurt

Temptations of The Flesh Part II

caused by someone you love. He will use himself as the topic of this open and honest session. He knows that he may have to step down from his church, but this is something that must be done.

He reached out to Mary but there was no response so he texted her and asked if she could come to church on Sunday, not as the first lady, just as a member of the congregation. It would be greatly appreciated if she could.

The bishop also reached out to Nena to ask the same of her, and to bring his son so he could introduce him to the church.

Nena quickly responded and said, "It's about time! Yes, we will be there."

The bishop knows he has to do a lot of soul searching because his life is about to change. He will be judge by his family, his church, and his community for his actions, but he knows that in order to get right with God he has to make a change. This would be one of the most important decisions he'd ever make - owning and taking accountability for his mistakes.

As the bishop was reaching out to Nena, she was lying next to Damon. Yes, they are still having sex with each other despite the warning Mary gave her. Damon wasn't about to tell her anything about his attraction for men. Besides, like he said, she was just a Kool pop.

James DeBoris Franklin Sr.

Damon saw the text the bishop sent and said, "Ok just be honest. Is this my child or is it his?"

"If I'm going to be honest, I really don't know. I was sleeping with both of you at that time. He helped me finically and you were fun and entertaining. I enjoyed both so yes, he could be either one of yours. Like you said, I'm just a Kool pop and you're just a Kool pod."

"Kool pod?" Damon questioned, "Oh! A Kool piece of dick!"

"Absolutely! For me this is all about having a good time with no connection or strings attached. I want what I want, when I want it, and you can get it when you need it. It's just that simple so don't make this complicated."

"I couldn't agree more. Now close your eyes and open your mouth. Allow your legs to relax to their natural position as I prepare you for my version of sixty-nine."

Nena did what was asked of her. Pleasure was given and received by both. Damon's phone started ringing but he didn't want to answer it because he was busy pleasing Nena, so he ignored it. It began to ring again and again, he ignored it. He heard it ding and knew whoever it was had left him a message, so he went back to giving her what she wanted.

Temptations of The Flesh Part II

After they finished, he read his text message. It was Darrius. He was rushed to the hospital because he had a fever, headaches, and muscle/joint aches along with a little dizziness. He wanted Damon to come to the hospital to check on him, but Damon was not interested in doing anything for or with Darrius. So, after reading his text, he deleted the message. He was still angry about how Darrius played him and how he interfered with Mary, so no he wasn't going anywhere near Darrius.

Darrius concluded that Damon wasn't coming to the hospital and that he was now on his own. The doctor told him it looked like he had a slight case of the flu, so he gave him some antibiotics along with instructions to take it easy and to get some rest.

Darrius was released and took an Uber home. Once at home, he noticed Damon was in his room. He never responded to his text, nor did he call so he now understands that it's over between them.

In the meantime, David had an awkward conversation with his mom about moving in with Mary. His mother didn't like it and advised him not to do it, but David was convinced that this was a great opportunity for him and his son to be a part of someone's life that loved them both. He told his mom not to worry because he believes he's making the right decision for them and that his decision was final. His mother reminded him that she would always be there for him, and Theo and they would forever have a home with her. David kissed his mother and thanked her for everything she had done to help him with his son. David called Mary and told her he had started packing their things. He told her that he was ready to share his life with her and that they would be ready soon.

Mary needed to tell David about the bishop wanting her to come to church Sunday, but she knew this was something she had to do alone. She needed to keep her and David a secret until her marriage was done. She believed David would understand but she just wanted to be open and honest with him about it.

David calls Mary and tells her that they are ready.

"Ok! I'm on my way" she says.

David begins to think about all of the good times he's had in his home. The night him and Tina shared a special moment under the stars. The love he received from his mother when Tina died, and Theo was born. He's grateful for the life he was given by his mother and now he's ready to be the man and father she has helped him to become.

As Mary arrives to pick up David and Theo, his mother greets her with a hug and whispers in her ear, "Take care of them because if you don't you will have me to answer to" kissing her on the cheek as she releases her.

Mary smiles and says, "I will."

Temptations of The Flesh Part II

David noticed Mary had a look of concern on her face as they drove off, so he asked, "What's wrong? What did my mother say to you?"

"She was just being a mom, but I have another surprise for you."

"Ok! I'm listening" David perked up.

"I really want to help you accomplish something that you would have done if this hadn't happened with Theo and that's to help you obtain your college degree. I'm going to pay for your schooling. You can now go get your engineering degree."

David was speechless, he couldn't believe she was going to help him go to school. He had given up on his dream of going to school but now Mary had made it possible. David was shocked by the news but was blown away when she pulled into their subdivision.

David looked at Mary. She just smiled and said, "Welcome home honey! This is an example of the life we are going to have together. Billy Ray said he would take of me, and he has. Theo has his own room, and we will raise him together."

David was so overwhelmed with joy he couldn't put his feelings into words, so he just loved her with hugs, kisses, and tears. "This is unbelievable! Thank you, Mary!

Mary tells David she had something to tell him, and he thinks it's another surprise, so he says excitedly, "OK what is it?"

Mary tells him about the bishop wanting her to come to church Sunday, but she needed to go without him.

"Mary, I trust you so if this is something you need to do, I'm going to support you. We are a family and you have made that clear. I'm going to stand with you on this" David consoled.

Mary believed that would've been his answer, but it was wonderful hearing him say it and showing his support for her. Mary kissed him and said thank you. She felt his appreciation for her rise up. She put Theo to bed because she knew what was coming.

David was in the kitchen waiting on her naked. He picks her up and sits her on the counter. He pulls her close and penetrates her. He stands up with her and pins her against the wall and begins to stroke harder. While her back was against the wall, he asked her to put her leg on his shoulder, then the other. He places his hands up under her butt and lifts her up so that his face is in the prefect position to give her head as he used the wall for leverage.

"Don't stop" Mary begs and grabs the back of David's head. "You're going to make me cum."

David takes her legs off his shoulders and carries her to the sofa. He puts her on her knees with her

Temptations of The Flesh Part II

back to him and penetrated her from behind. Once he pushed all of himself inside of her, he put his arm around her neck and held her body close to his and said, "Baby! I want to feel your body tremble as you let your love for me flow. I'll give you all of me and I mean every inch of me. Can you feel it?"

While David was deep inside of her, Mary began to squeeze his penis. This made him push deeper and Mary couldn't control her body. The deeper he penetrated, the weaker she got. Mary felt David swell up inside her, so she knew he was about to explode. She started to ride David fast and hard until their bodies locked up and they had the most beautiful orgasm either one had ever experienced.

"That was amazing! If we keep going at it like this, you're going to get me pregnant" Mary says.

"I wouldn't have a problem with that. Would you?"

"Absolutely not" Mary replied.

They made their way to the bedroom where they got comfortable and had another round of a delightfully pleasing sex. They couldn't believe the most memorable moments in their new home, on the first night, would be how they blessed the kitchen, living room, and their bedroom all in the same night.

Mary was not used to this type of sexual activity, but she knew David was young and full of energy. This type of love making was going to be part of their lives: she was exhausted but completely satisfied. As she lay in David's arms, she feels a level of comfort that she never got from the bishop. She knew what she had with David was genuine. She was in her safe space with him and knew she had made the right decision by making David her one and only.

A new day had dawned, and it was Sunday. Mary woke up happy and proceeded to get ready for church. She was a little nervous about going without being the first lady but she's dealing with it.

As she pulls up at the church, she sees Nena walking in with her son. She's now curious about what the bishop is plotting. As she sits in her car, she contemplates not going in because it seems like this is going to get messy. She decides to go in and as she gets to the entrance, she is greeted by the mothers of the church. They tried to escort her to her seat, and she respectfully refused. They again asked her to take her seat as first lady of the church and she refused once more.

Mary sat at the back of the church. Just in case things started to get out of hand, she could leave quickly and gracefully. The bishop sent one of his deacons to go get his son from Nena to bring him into his chambers. Shortly after that, he came out holding his son's hand. The congregation was a little uneasy because of the rumors floating around about him. Bishop White informed the church that today was going to be about revealing the truth.

Temptations of The Flesh Part II

"It's not the topic of a sermon, it's about me coming clean about who I am and the wrong I've done." He apologized to the church, Mary, and the community. He informed them that Mary had asked for a divorce because of his infidelity and the little boy standing next to him was his son. He asked Nena to stand up and he informed the church that this was his son's mother. Some were surprised but most weren't. He explained that the things he did were very disrespectful to his soon-to-be ex-wife and the church. He asked for forgiveness from both and expressed sorrow for the damage he caused. He also wanted to let the church know that he didn't want to leave but understood if they elected to release him from his duties as the pastor of the church. The congregation was starting to get disruptive.

A woman in the congregation stood up and said, "I am currently with child and Bishop White is the father."

The bishop's face did not appear to be shocked. He did not disagree with the woman and said, "I can't say that I'm not the father because I know I have done things to make that possible so once again please forgive me."

Mary wasn't surprised and neither was Nena. Mary knew her decision to let the bishop go was the best she could've made. She waved goodbye to the bishop as she exited the church with a smile of joy mixed with a little bit of hurt and pain.

The bishop and his son went back to his chambers and Nena followed them.

"I knew you was sleeping with other women and now you have another baby on the way. All I have to say about that is you better keep that money and those house calls coming because if you don't, I can promise you that you will receive a package that will change your life and the package I'm speaking of is called child support because for me It just got personal." Nena took her son from the bishop and walked out of his office.

The deacons entered his office and closed the door to discuss his actions as well as his future with the church. It doesn't look good for the bishop.

As Nena leaves the parking lot of the church, she calls Damon and asked him to meet her at her place because she was in need of his sexual activities to help release the stress Bishop White has caused. Damon was more than happy to assist her with her needs.

Damon noticed he hadn't seen a lot of Darrius and began to have some concerns about him. He goes to knock on his door.

"It's open" Darrius answers. Damon sees Darrius curled up in his bed as if he was in pain. "What is it? What do you want?

Temptations of The Flesh Part II

"I was just checking on you. You good?" Damon asks.

"Yes! I'm great now leave me alone" Darrius responds.

Damon slams the door and says, "You will never have to worry about me checking on you again."

As Damon leaves the apartment, Darrius knew he needed his help because his condition seems to have gotten worse. Because Damon had ghosted him the last time he needed him, he allowed his pride to take over, wishing Damon away.

On Mary's drive home, she receives a phone call from David asking what time she thought she'd be back from church. Mary told him that she was almost at home, and she would see him soon. David had cooked for her and Theo to show his love and appreciation for her. As she walked into the house, she could smell the food that he had prepared but before she could greet David she ran to the bathroom and threw up. She was so embarrassed. She apologized to him and told him that she could not eat anything right now but maybe later when she starts to feel better. David understood and catered to all of Mary's needs.

Mary dozes off and doesn't wake up until the next day. She begins to reflect on why she might be feeling sick. The first thing that comes to mind is her interaction with Damon and what she could possibly be faced with and that scares her. She knows her test was negative, but she also knows there's a chance that her results could change so she's contemplating taking another test.

Mary started to think about all the sex she and David have been having and wonders if she might be pregnant. She quickly disregarded that thought because of the length of their relationship.

While she was deep in thought, her phone rang. It was her doctor's office. Mary answers and his office tells her that she needs to come in because they have some important information for her. She asked if they could tell her what it was over the phone, and she was told no, the doctor wanted to see her. That made Mary nervous and now her mind is racing with the question of what was so important that she had to come into the office. Just as she started to calm down, they asked her if she could bring her husband as well. That just confirmed it for her. It's clear that the results from their STD tests have changed and one or both has been found to have a sexually transmitted disease. She's in panic mode because she thought all was well. She had been sleeping with David unprotected so he could also be infected.

Mary can't get control of her thoughts. This can't be happening. The test results were negative. How am I going to tell this man that I might have given him the very same disease that his son has. David walks

Temptations of The Flesh Part II

into the room and notices that Mary was upset and had been crying. He asked her what was wrong, but Mary didn't answer. He asked her again.

"I'll tell you later. I have a doctor's appointment that I must go to and when I return, I will tell you what's going on but for now please give me a little space so I can think and process things" Mary replied.

Reluctantly, David agreed and reassured her that regardless of what's happening he would support her through it all. That gave Mary a good feeling but depending on what the doctor had to say his support for her might turn into uncontrollable anger.

On her way to see the doctor she calls Bishop White. He did not answer, and she didn't leave him a message. She continued to her appointment with hopes of her being wrong about what she thought it might be.

When she arrived for her appointment, the nurse asked if her husband would be joining them.

"No!" Mary said firmly.

The nurse proceeded to take Mary to her assigned room. Once inside she told Mary that the doctor would be with her shortly.

The doctor finally comes in and he asked Mary if her husband would be joining.

"He will not be joining us today" Mary replied.

James DeBoris Franklin Sr.

The doctor tells her that he really wishes he could come because he needs to be present for the information he has to share. He asks if she could try to call him again.

Mary tries to contact the bishop and again no answer.

"What is going on and why is it so important that my husband needs to be here with me? Just tell me! What is it?" The doctor looks at Mary and begins to smile. Mary says, "Why are you smiling at me?"

The doctor tells her that he really wanted to tell them both but since the bishop wasn't going to make it to the appointment, he would just tell her.

"Tell me what!" Mary demands.

"Mary! You and your husband are with child. You are pregnant!" the doctor exclaims.

"Pregnant!"

"Yes! Pregnant that's why I wanted him here with you so you both could share in this life changing news."

Mary was shocked but also relieved. Mary appeared to be happy, but her mind was working overtime, she had gone from one problem to another.

Mary thanked the doctor and his staff and asked them not to share this news with her husband because she wanted to surprise him with it.

Temptations of The Flesh Part II

Mary is still married to the bishop while living with David and Theo. Now, she's pregnant and does not know who the baby's father is. Mary looked at her situation that was brought on by her husband's betrayal as a time to return the favor. *Do unto him as he has done unto me. It's payback time.* She allowed her hurt and anger to put her on a course of disrespecting herself. She wanted to make him pay for causing her all this grief so she made decisions that could have ruined her life. She couldn't comprehend what was really happening as she was going through it. She blamed it on being angry, because she had held it down for her husband while playing blind and acting like she didn't see or know what he was doing when all along she knew. She just loved him so much that she made herself numb to it. She now understands how hurt and pain can cause you to become something and somebody that you're not. She had to take a long look at herself and has concluded that the only reason she moved the way she did was because she made it personal.

The End.

Made in the USA
Columbia, SC
04 November 2024

45648124R00041